D1135500

CHILDREN'S STORYTIME TREASURY

Aesop's Fables

A PARRAGON BOOK

PUBLISHED BY PARRAGON BOOK SERVICE LTD.
UNITS 13-17, AVONBRIDGE TRADING ESTATE, ATLANTIC ROAD,
AVONMOUTH, BRISTOL BS11 9QD

PRODUCED BY THE TEMPLAR COMPANY PLC,
PIPPBROOK MILL, LONDON ROAD, DORKING, SURREY RH4 1JE

COPYRIGHT © 1996 PARRAGON BOOK SERVICE LIMITED

DESIGNED BY MARK KINGSLEY-MONKS

ILLUSTRATED BY LORNA HUSSEY

PRINTED AND BOUND IN SPAIN

ISBN 0-75252-033-4

CHILDREN'S STORYTIME TREASURY

Aesop's Fables

PARRAGON

The Town Mouse and the Country Mouse

O nce upon a time there were two little mice. One mouse was very grand and lived in the town but the other was quite different. He was a Country Mouse. He lived under the roots of an old oak tree in a small hole lined with straw and dry grass. He slept on a scrap of sheep's wool and wore a brown waistcoat he had made himself from an old grainsack.

"How lucky I am to live here," the Country Mouse said to himself. "I must invite my cousin to come and share my cosy home," but when the smart Town Mouse arrived, he looked about the little hole in dismay. What a shabby home! The Country Mouse laughed and led him to a table piled high with food.

"I have prepared a special meal," he said excitedly. "A cob of corn, fresh hazelnuts and rosy red rosehips."

But the Town Mouse wrinkled his nose in disgust.

"I cannot eat this food," he protested. "You must come and stay with me and discover what real food is like." So the next day the Country Mouse returned with the Town Mouse to his home in the big, busy city.

"This is what a home should be like," said the Town Mouse proudly as he led the Country Mouse from room to room. "I like soft carpets and comfortable furniture. There are no leaves or mud here."

Soon they were hungry. "Follow me," said the Town Mouse, "but there will be no rosehips or hazlenuts on the menu!" he added with a twinkle in his eye. The little Country Mouse gasped when he saw the wonderful spread laid out on the large dining table.

"This is *real* food," cried the Town Mouse. "Let us begin!" but as soon as he scampered across the floor two large dogs came bounding into the room, barking fiercely and the Country Mouse drew back in terror.

"I'm going back to my home!" he told his cousin. "You may sleep on a soft duck-down mattress under a satin quilt while I have only a scrap of wool for my bed. You may wear a red velvet coat with gold

buttons while my clothes are patched and darned. You may feast on roast beef and chocolate cake while I live off the nuts and berries of the hedgerow. You can enjoy the excitement of the town if you wish but give me the plain and simple life any time!"

AND THE MORAL OF THIS STORY IS:

BETTER A POOR AND CAREFREE LIFE

THAN A RICH AND WORRIED LIFE

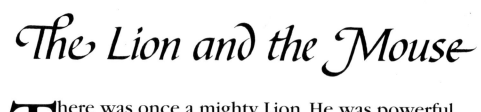

The Lion and the Mouse

There was once a mighty Lion. He was powerful and strong and when he roared, the earth shook, the parrots squawked and the monkeys ran chattering to the treetops.

All the animals were afraid of him and they called him the King of the Beasts. The little Mouse was especially frightened of the Lion for she knew that if one of his paws landed on top of her, she would be squashed as flat as a blade of grass. She tried her best to keep well away from the King of the Beasts.

One day, as the Lion slept in the shade of an old acacia tree, the Mouse was scuttling busily about her business, searching for small seeds to eat. Little did she know that her scurrying steps took her close by the sleeping Lion. Up his leg she scampered, all the time thinking he was nothing but a smooth termite hill. But as her feet ran tickling across his back the Lion awoke with a mighty roar. The little mouse tumbled to the ground and in a flash he had trapped her tail under one enormous paw.

"What is the meaning of this?" he rumbled and the Mouse shook with fright. "Do you not know who I am?"

The little Mouse could feel his hot breath singeing her whiskers and she nodded her head up and down rapidly.

"Yes, yes!" she gasped. "You are the King of the Beasts, the Lord of the Jungle, the mighty Lion."

"That is so," smiled the Lion approvingly. "Just so," and he tightened his grip on her tail.

"Oh, please have pity on me," the Mouse begged. "If you save my life today why, who knows, perhaps one day I shall save yours."

The Lion threw back his head and laughed and laughed. "*You* save *my* life?" he said. "A little Mouse save the King of the Beasts? That I should certainly like to see."

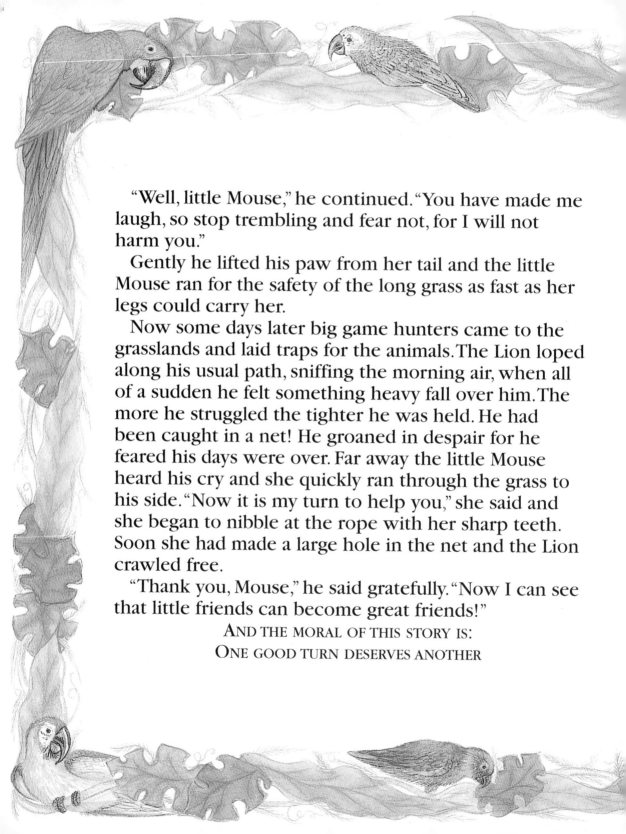

"Well, little Mouse," he continued. "You have made me laugh, so stop trembling and fear not, for I will not harm you."

Gently he lifted his paw from her tail and the little Mouse ran for the safety of the long grass as fast as her legs could carry her.

Now some days later big game hunters came to the grasslands and laid traps for the animals. The Lion loped along his usual path, sniffing the morning air, when all of a sudden he felt something heavy fall over him. The more he struggled the tighter he was held. He had been caught in a net! He groaned in despair for he feared his days were over. Far away the little Mouse heard his cry and she quickly ran through the grass to his side. "Now it is my turn to help you," she said and she began to nibble at the rope with her sharp teeth. Soon she had made a large hole in the net and the Lion crawled free.

"Thank you, Mouse," he said gratefully. "Now I can see that little friends can become great friends!"

AND THE MORAL OF THIS STORY IS:

ONE GOOD TURN DESERVES ANOTHER

The Fox and the Crow

There was once a fine Fox. He had a glossy red coat and a beautiful bushy tail. His pointed ears pricked up at the smallest sound and his sharp nose twitched at the faintest smell.

Early one evening as the Fox prowled under the old oak trees, his black nose began to prickle.

"What a wonderful smell!" said the Fox to himself. "It is better than rabbits. It is better than chickens. What could it be?" He bent his head to the ground and snuffled amongst the leaves and the grass. The tantalising smell was not down there. He sniffed again. "Where is this marvellous smell coming from?" he puzzled. He raised his nose high in the air and sniffed once more. Then he caught sight of something perched high above him on the branch of an oak tree.

It was a glossy black crow and she was holding something in her beak. Something yellow. Something tasty. Something very like cheese!

The Fox licked his lips. He badly wanted that piece of cheese. But how was he to reach it for he certainly could not jump high enough to catch the bird?

Then the cunning Fox had a clever idea. He looked up at the Crow and the Crow looked down at him.

"What a magnificent bird!" exclaimed the Fox. "Such glossy black feathers. Such a bright yellow beak."

The Crow stood quite still but she quivered with pleasure to hear the Fox's charming words.

"What sparkling eyes!" continued the Fox. "They glitter like two beads of jet. I cannot believe there is a bird anywhere in the world who could match this beautiful Crow." The Crow had never heard such flattery and she fluffed up her feathers and bobbed up and down on the branch, drinking in the bold Fox's honeyed words. Then the Fox spoke again and his eyes never left the large piece of cheese.

"I wonder if the Crow's voice is as splendid as her appearance," he said. "She would indeed be Queen of all the Birds if such a wondrous bird was also blessed with a glorious singing voice."

Then the vain Crow could not resist the chance to show off and opening her mouth wide, she began to caw loudly. Well, the wily Fox knew just what would happen next and he was waiting!

The cheese tumbled from the Crow's beak and fell straight into the Fox's open mouth. He chewed it slowly and lovingly and at last swallowed it with a happy sigh.

"Very tasty," he said, and he licked his lips as the Crow screeched with rage above his head.

"Well," said the Fox smugly. "So you *do* have a voice. My, but what a pity it is that you were not blessed with a brain!" and he sauntered off with his tail held high in the air.

AND THE MORAL OF THIS STORY IS:

NEVER TRUST A FLATTERER

The Hare and the Tortoise

There once lived a most bold and bumptious Hare. He loved to stroll around the warren with his nose held high in the air, and it was evident to one and all that this Hare considered himself to be the finest Hare in all the land. Now there was one thing that the Hare was proud of above all else. He had been blessed with strong back legs and that meant he could run like the wind. He never missed an opportunity to show off his running skills to his friends and no-one had ever been known to beat him. Or not until the day he met the Tortoise, who slowly crawled by as the Hare was bragging to his friends.

"Hurry up, hurry up, old Tortoise!" laughed the Hare. "If you went much slower the grass would grow over you!" The Tortoise stared at him coolly.

"You may rush about all you wish," he said, "but I get to where I want to be soon enough, thank you." He looked the Hare up and down slowly before continuing. "In fact, I reckon I could get there quicker than you, fast as you are." The Hare burst out laughing.

"Quicker than me? That I should like to see!" and so he challenged the Tortoise to a race.

The arrangements were soon made and the very next day everyone turned out to watch the Hare and the Tortoise run their race.

"Five, four, three, two, one, go!" cried the Fox, who was acting as umpire, and in a flash the Hare was out of sight and over the hill. The crowd clapped and cheered as the old Tortoise lifted first one foot and then the other and slowly began to make his way along the path. He looked neither right nor left but kept his eyes on the winding road straight ahead.

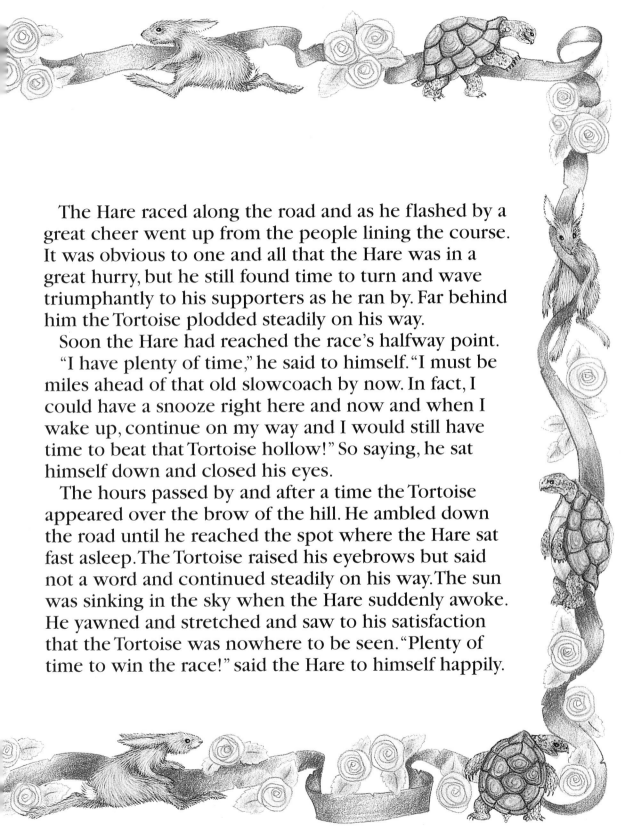

The Hare raced along the road and as he flashed by a great cheer went up from the people lining the course. It was obvious to one and all that the Hare was in a great hurry, but he still found time to turn and wave triumphantly to his supporters as he ran by. Far behind him the Tortoise plodded steadily on his way.

Soon the Hare had reached the race's halfway point.

"I have plenty of time," he said to himself. "I must be miles ahead of that old slowcoach by now. In fact, I could have a snooze right here and now and when I wake up, continue on my way and I would still have time to beat that Tortoise hollow!" So saying, he sat himself down and closed his eyes.

The hours passed by and after a time the Tortoise appeared over the brow of the hill. He ambled down the road until he reached the spot where the Hare sat fast asleep. The Tortoise raised his eyebrows but said not a word and continued steadily on his way. The sun was sinking in the sky when the Hare suddenly awoke. He yawned and stretched and saw to his satisfaction that the Tortoise was nowhere to be seen. "Plenty of time to win the race!" said the Hare to himself happily.

Off down the road he sped but as he came over the brow of the hill he saw the most amazing sight. There ahead of him was the Tortoise taking his last few steps towards the finish line! The crowds cheered wildly as his shiny shell broke the tape in two and the Fox declared him the winner. As the Hare panted for breath at the end of the race, the Tortoise smiled placidly. "Slow I may be but I keep my eye on the goal and I don't let anything distract me!"

AND THE MORAL OF THIS STORY IS:
SLOW AND STEADY WINS THE RACE

The Fox and the Stork

One day a Fox decided to invite a Stork to tea. He made all the preparations in the kitchen and set the table with his best crockery. He brushed his fine long tail until it shone like copper and then dressed in his best blue coat.

Soon there was a tap, tap, tap upon the door. It was the Stork and with a great flourish, the Fox opened the door and bowed low.

"Do step inside," he cried. "Welcome to my humble home." The Stork looked very elegant in a beautiful purple hat and matching cape and as she stepped daintily into the room her hat feathers quivered. She was very hungry. "I do hope the Fox has plenty of food," she said to herself anxiously.

"I have cooked some beautiful soup," announced the Fox. "Let us begin," and he showed the Stork to a chair. But the poor Stork was dismayed to see that the only plates laid upon the table were quite flat. How would she be able to eat off such a dish?

The Fox came bustling in from the kitchen and carefully set a steaming pot of soup down in the centre of the table.

The Fox ladled out the soup with much smacking of lips and many appreciative sniffs. Then he sat down, lifted his spoon and smiled broadly at the Stork.

"Do tuck in!" he urged. "This is my best soup!"

But the Stork looked down at her plate and sighed unhappily. She could not swallow this soup with her long pointed beak and so she could only sit and watch as the Fox greedily lapped up his plateful.

When the Fox had quite finished he looked across at the Stork in surprise.

"Did you not enjoy the soup?" he asked, wrinkling his brow as if greatly concerned. But the poor Stork was too polite to complain and so the wily Fox lapped up her portion as well.

The next day when the Stork awoke she was still hungry. She decided to repay the Fox's hospitality and invited him to dinner that evening. He was delighted and accepted eagerly.

But as the Fox sat down to eat at the Stork's table he could hardly believe his eyes. The only dishes upon the table were two tall jugs! The Stork dipped her slender beak inside the jug and drank her soup but the Fox could only lick his lips hungrily and watch, for there was no way he could get at the food.

He returned home a sadder and wiser Fox with nobody to blame but himself for, as he plainly realised, he had only been paid back for his own uncaring behaviour.

AND THE MORAL OF THIS STORY IS:
DO AS YOU WOULD BE DONE BY

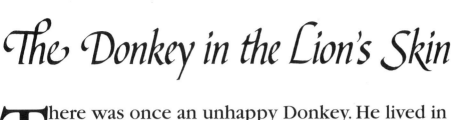

The Donkey in the Lion's Skin

There was once an unhappy Donkey. He lived in the jungle with all the other animals but they were cruel and often made fun of him. How he wished he could get his own back on the unfriendly creatures but whenever they saw him they just laughed and called him rude names.

One day the Donkey had quite a fright. As he trotted along the jungle path he thought he saw a Lion waiting to pounce on him. But the Lion didn't move and then the Donkey realised that it was not a real Lion after all, but just a Lion's skin.

"This would make a fine costume for me to wear," said the Donkey and he slipped it over his back. He looked exactly like a real Lion!

"Now I can teach those animals a lesson," said the Donkey, and he hid in a thicket and waited for someone to pass by. Soon the Monkey came swinging along, clinging to the vines with his tail. Out jumped the Donkey with a fierce roar and the Monkey ran screeching up a tree. Then the Bear came ambling along the path but when he saw the Lion he ran whimpering into the bushes.

Then the fierce Tiger came prowling by but when the Donkey jumped out at him, he ran off into the jungle as fast as he could. The happy Donkey had never had so much fun in all his life! He stamped his hooves with glee and rocked with silent laughter.

The sun was slowly sinking in the west as the crafty Fox slunk into view. With his head bent low, he sniffed for food amongst the shrubs and grasses. He could smell all sorts of interesting things, but he could not smell danger so imagine his surprise when out rushed the Donkey in the Lion's skin! To the Donkey's great delight the terrified Fox yelped and ran for cover with his tail between his legs.

But this time the silly Donkey could not help himself and he laughed out loud. His loud bray echoed through the jungle and the wily Fox stood stock still. Slowly he walked back to the fierce Lion skin and looked under the great head. There he came face to face with the embarrassed Donkey and the silly animal hung his head low.

The Fox laughed long and loud and then all the other animals came running.

The astonished creatures gathered around the blushing Donkey and soon the jungle rang to the sounds of their catcalls and hoots of glee.

"Why, it wasn't a fierce Lion who pounced out on me after all!" cried the Monkey. "It was just the silly old Donkey," grumbled the Bear.

The Donkey looked very ashamed.

"You foolish Donkey!" said the Fox. "If only you had kept your moth shut, your trick might well have succeeded but you just had to give your game away with your loud bray!"

AND THE MORAL OF THIS STORY IS:

A FOOL MAY DECEIVE OTHERS WITH HIS APPEARANCE BUT HIS WORDS WILL SOON REVEAL HIM

The Fox without a Tail

There was once a fine Fox, a most handsome fellow with a shiny red coat and a long bushy tail. This Fox was a rather vain creature and he spent long hours brushing his tail from top to tip until it shone like bright copper.

But one evening he had a most dreadful accident. As he hunted amongst the thickets and hedgerows for a tasty meal he suddenly heard a loud *clack!* and felt the most dreadful pain.

He realised at once that he had been caught in a trap and, pull as he might, his beautiful tail was stuck fast. Suddenly the pain stopped and to his great dismay the Fox found his tail lying in all its glory upon the ground. The trap had pulled it clean off. This was a calamity! Why, he was a Fox! The best and finest Fox that ever was — and what was a Fox without his tail? Why, little more than a laughing stock! How the other Foxes would taunt him when they saw him creeping by, tail-less. The very thought of it was more than he could bear.

After a while he stood up, collected his hat and made his way to the forest dell where the Foxes met for their nightly meetings. As the Fox strutted into the centre of the circle a hushed silence fell on the entire company. He wore his best hat and tucked inside the hatband was his own fine red tail!

A young Fox began to titter, then another, then another and soon the forest rang to the sounds of their rude laughter. With a dignified expression, the Fox held up his hand for silence and spoke.

"As you know, I have been blessed with a particularly fine specimen of a tail and I have been proud to carry it around behind me ever since I was born. But now I feel the time has come for a change. Tails should not drag behind us in the dirt. No, they should be worn on high, where their beauty can be fully admired."

The Fox paraded around the glade.

"This is the new fashion" he said "so you had all better start wearing your tails on your hats, like me."

Then an old Fox stood creakily to his feet.

"We have heard what you have to say, Brother Fox, but answer me this," he said. "Would you be quite so keen for us to follow this new fashion if your own tail had not been pulled off in a trap?" Then the poor Fox saw that everyone had seen through his cunning plan and he slunk off into the forest, much ashamed.

AND THE MORAL OF THIS STORY IS:

IF YOU SUFFER SOME MISFORTUNE, MAKE THE BEST OF
WHAT YOU HAVE AND DO NOT TRY TO
MAKE OTHERS SUFFER ALSO

The Wolf and the Ass

One day the Ass set off to find some sweet grass to eat. He followed the path from the jungle and soon found himself far away from his usual haunts. Here the grass was lush and green and soon the Ass was busy chewing away, quite contented and without a care in the world.

But as he munched happily in the meadow a big grey Wolf crept up on him unawares. Suddenly the Ass pricked up his ears for he could hear the pad of soft paws behind him.

"That Wolf means to make me his supper!" said the Donkey to himself.

When the Wolf was close enough to pounce, the Ass lifted his head and called out quite calmly.

"I shouldn't do that if I was you," he said. The Wolf was astonished. Why was the Ass so unafraid?

"I have trodden on a sharp thorn," explained the Ass, "and if you eat me it will be sure to stick in your throat. I am sure you wouldn't want that."

The Wolf shook his head and the Ass continued.

"I will lift up my hoof and then you can pull out the thorn before you eat me," he offered helpfully. The Wolf could not believe his luck. He stood behind the Ass and as the Ass waited patiently with his hoof in the air, the Wolf had a good look for the thorn. But there was no thorn to be found!

Then the Ass summoned up all his strength and with a loud and triumphant whinny he gave a mighty kick. The Wolf flew head over heels into the air and landed in the middle of a thorn bush, howling with pain.

"That Ass is not as stupid as he looks," thought the Wolf to himself as he picked the thorns from his bottom, one by one, but the Ass just smiled at him sweetly as he trotted off home.

AND THE MORAL OF THIS STORY IS:
BEWARE OF UNEXPECTED FAVOURS

The Dog and his Reflection

There was once a naughty Dog. He loved to sit outside the Butcher's shop and admire the strings of shiny sausages and rows of pink pork chops. How he wished he could help himself to something to eat!

One day when the Butcher's back was turned, the Dog ran into the shop and seized a large ham bone in his strong teeth. Off down the street he ran while the Butcher waved his sharpest knife and shouted after him angrily.

"Nobody has a bone as big and as tasty as mine!" the
Dog said to himself as he set off for home. But as he
crossed the bridge what should he see but another
Dog with another bone — and this bone was just as
big as his own! The Dog was astonished.

"I shall have that bone," he decided. "Two bones are
better than one!" With that, the silly Dog opened his
mouth and snapped greedily.

But what a shock he got when his own bone
tumbled from his mouth and landed with a splash in
the water. To the Dog's great dismay the bone sank
quickly out of sight and he realised he was left with

nothing at all. Slowly he trudged back to his kennel, feeling very sorry for himself. He lay down and rested his head upon his paws. What a tragedy it was to have something in your grasp and then have it snatched suddenly away.

"I was wrong," sighed the Dog unhappily. "One bone is much, much better than none."

AND THE MORAL OF THIS STORY IS:

BE GRATEFUL FOR WHAT YOU HAVE

OTHER TITLES IN THIS SERIES INCLUDE:

GRIMM'S FAIRYTALES

HANS ANDERSEN'S FAIRYTALES

JUST-SO STORIES

NURSERY TALES

TALES FROM THE ARABIAN NIGHTS

TALES OF BRER RABBIT

WIND IN THE WILLOWS